meg
GOLDBERG
on Parade

To Avital, my fabulous first-
born and keen-eyed critic,
and to Yudi, for making
every day so much fun
– A.W.R.

To my wife and sons
– C.L.

Text copyright © 2015 by Andria Warmflash Rosenbaum
Illustrations copyright © 2015 by Lerner Publishing Group, Inc.

KAR-BEN PUBLISHING
A division of Lerner Publishing Group, Inc.
241 First Avenue North
Minneapolis, MN 55401 USA
1-800-4-KARBEN

Website address: www.karben.com

Main body text set in Fink Heavy.
Typeface provided by House Industries.

Cataloging-in-Publication Data on file with the Library of Congress

Rosenbaum, Andria Warmflash, 1958-
    Meg Goldberg on parade / by Andria Warmflash Rosenbaum ; illustrated by Christopher Lyles.
      pages   cm
    Summary: A young girl attends the Celebrate Israel Parade in New York City, where she is
crowned Grand Marshal.
    ISBN: 978-1-4677-3906-1 (lib. bdg. : alk. paper)
    [1. Stories in rhyme. 2. Parades—Fiction. 3. Israel—Fiction.] I. Lyles, Christopher, 1977-
illustrator. II. Title.
PZ8.3.R72245Me 2015
[E]—dc23   2014029041

Manufactured in the United States of America
1 - CG - 12/31/14

meg GOLDBERG on Parade

By Andria Warmflash Rosenbaum
Illustrated by Christopher Lyles

KAR-BEN
PUBLISHING

One Sunday the Goldbergs,
who lived in Pine Ridge,
drove into the city,
just over the bridge.

They parked and then walked to a spot in the shade,
to spend the day watching the Israel Parade!

Meg waited and wondered if there would be floats,
musical marching bands wearing blue coats,
juggling jesters with quick, moving hands,
who might need some help
from a girl in the stands.

She pictured herself as a part of it all,
even though she was quite timid and small.

The wind swept her up,
as her dreams held her high.
The marching began...
Meg decided to try...

First came the mayor, with Meg to his right,
past the Plaza Hotel and through a red light.
She shared her umbrella to block out the sun.
"Thanks, Meg," he said. "I was feeling well-done."

Children came next with balloons on long strings,
and with posters of places and Israeli things.

Floating on air,
Meg tossed samples for free,
of couscous and pita
and sweet, minty tea.

She folk-danced with ladies
who stepped to the beat,
while leaping in line
just past 61st Street.

She carried an Israeli flag, blue and white,
and clung to it tightly with all of her might.

"*WHIRRR*" purred an airplane
on one of the floats,
as Meg led a group
playing Yemenite notes.

Aliyah-niks waved and called out, "Shalom!
Come for a visit! You'll feel right at home."

Slow-moving camels roamed 5th Avenue,
sneaking a peek at the Central Park Zoo.
Guiding the herd with a grin and a wave,
Meg Goldberg was growing a little bit brave.

She hummed "Hatikvah" while walking on stilts,

and played it on bagpipes, with men wearing kilts.

Majorette Meg steered
a booming brass band,
with all of New York
at her humble command.

Every policeman Meg met on the route,
was given a "Thank you" and then a salute.

They crowned her Grand Marshal
and made it quite clear,
they needed Meg back
for the following year.

WHOOSH went the wind, raining dust everywhere.
It spun Meg around as it tangled her hair.

She opened her eyes. Traffic started to flow.
"Meg," said her mom. "It's all over. Let's go."

Through dinner, and bath, she remembered the fun,
of all the things she'd imagined she'd done.

She counted the many
new friends she had made,

while marching along
in the Israel Parade.

At last Mrs. Goldberg found time to unwind,
to rest her sore feet and to quiet her mind.
But she found a surprise when she tried to sit down—
and landed on top of a shiny, gold CROWN!

Glossary

Aliyah-niks: people who move to live in Israel

Grand Marshal: a person in charge of a ceremony

Hatikvah: Israel's national anthem

Shalom: Hebrew for hello, goodbye, and peace

Yemenite: from Yemen, an Arab country in the Middle East, which has influenced Jewish and Israeli culture

Author's Note

The annual Celebrate Israel Parade, begun in 1964, is held every spring in the heart of New York City. Over thirty thousand marchers stroll up Fifth Avenue. The parade showcases groups from elementary schools, high schools, yeshivot, synagogues, Jewish community centers, and many other Jewish institutions. Colorful floats, award winning marching bands, politicians, and entertainers also participate in the parade, showing their support for Israel. Tens of thousands of spectators cheer on the sidelines. The Celebrate Israel Parade is a colossal party, graciously hosted by New York City.